ACKNOWLEDGMENT is made for permission to adapt material from the following:
Angling in America, by Charles Eliot Goodspeed. Copyright 1939 by Charles E. Goodspeed.
Houghton Mifflin Company. ("A Pet Trout")
The Origin of the Celebrated Jumping Frog of Calaveras County, by Oscar Lewis. Copyright 1931 by
The Book Club of California. ("The Jumping Frog")
"The Saga of Pecos Bill," by Edward O'Reilly. *The Century Magazine*. Copyright 1923 by
The Century Company. ("A Tale of Pecos Bill")
Paul Bunyan and His Big Blue Ox, by W.B. Laughead. Red River Lumber Company, Westwood,
California, 1940. ("Paul Bunyan and the Little Blue Ox")
Paul Bunyan and Natural History, by Charles Edward Brown. Madison, Wisconsin, 1935.
("Paul Bunyan's Natural History")
"That Rabbit That Wouldn't Help Dig the Well," contributed by Miss Dora Lee Newman to a book
called *Marion County in the Making*. Fairmont, Marion County, West Virginia, 1918.
Privately printed. ("The Tar Man")
Stories and Speeches of William O. Bradley. Copyright 1916 by Transylvania Printing Company.
("The Squirrels and the Corn" and "Capturing a Young Eagle")
Folklore from Maryland, collected by Annie Weston Whitney and Caroline Canfield Bullock.
Memoirs of the American Folklore Society, volume XVIII, 1925. ("The Singing Geese")
Stars Fell on Alabama, by Carl Carmer. Copyright © 1934 by Carl Carmer. Farrar and Rinehart, Inc.
("The Knee-High Man")

Library of Congress Cataloging-in-Publication Data Available

Lot #: 10 9 8 7 6 5 4 3 2 1
04/10
Published by Sterling Publishing Co., Inc.
387 Park Avenue South, New York, NY 10016
New text © 2010 by Sterling Publishing Co., Inc
Adapted from material previously published and © 1961
by Doubleday & Company, Inc., Garden City, New York
Distributed in Canada by Sterling Publishing
^c/o Canadian Manda Group, 165 Dufferin Street
Toronto, Ontario, Canada M6K 3H6
Distributed in the United Kingdom by GMC Distribution Services
Castle Place, 166 High Street, Lewes, East Sussex, England BN7 1XU
Distributed in Australia by Capricorn Link (Australia) Pty. Ltd.
P.O. Box 704, Windsor, NSW 2756, Australia

Sterling ISBN 978-1-4027-7322-8

For information about custom editions, special sales, premium and
corporate purchases, please contact Sterling Special Sales
Department at 800-805-5489 or specialsales@sterlingpublishing.com

Designed by Kate Moll

Animal Folk Tales of America

PAUL BUNYAN, PECOS BILL, THE JUMPING FROG, DAVY CROCKETT, JOHNNY APPLESEED, SWEET BETSY, AND MANY OTHERS

Adapted and illustrated by Caldecott Honor-winner

TONY PALAZZO

STERLING

New York / London
www.sterlingpublishing.com/kids

Contents

INTRODUCTION

THE FOLK TALES OF AMERICA are filled with legends and fantasies and exaggerations. In a new country demanding hard work and wisdom of its pioneers, these stories captured that pioneering spirit of courage and hope. This spirit that was a very real part of everyday life.

From the days of the pioneers—and even long before—life in this land was closely connected with the animals that shared it. Whether the setting was forest or plain, lake or stream, human survival depended on maintaining a respectful relationship with wild creatures.

Celebrating the ingenious, amusing, and sometimes outrageous animals that enlivened the early American experience, this retelling of some of our favorite folk tales can highlight for a new generation of young readers an important legacy of our national folklore: understanding our kinship with the natural world.

These folk tales remind us of a time in our history, not really so long ago, when every journey held the promise of new discoveries—an uncharted mountain, an unexplored river—even a blue ox! Today, as we travel across the nation on jets and superhighways, it's good to glance backward even as we fly ever forward.

THE FISH OUT OF WATER

TOMMY was a trout who once got himself stranded on the dry bank of a creek. He was rescued by a young scout who took him home to his village and kept him in a rain barrel.

Tommy and his rescuer became good friends. Soon the scout even taught the grateful trout to leap right out of the rain barrel and follow him across the wet grass.

In time it appeared that, unlike any ordinary fish, Tommy did not even need water.

On fine days the pair took long hikes together, Tommy swishing through the wet grass beside the moccasins of his friend. Could it be that the trout had truly become a land fish?

One day, a walk brought them to a bridge. The scout crossed the bridge first and then, realizing that the fish had not followed him across, peered over the edge. Sure enough, there was Tommy, swimming in the clear, sparkling water below. With a splash of his rainbow-colored tail, Tommy waved good-bye and hurried downstream, and the scout smiled to know that he had helped a friend find his way back home.

THE BEAR
AND
THE LUMBERJACK

ANNABEL was a bear who loved honey so much she would even climb a rainbow to get some.

Her owner was a lumberjack, and though he didn't have rainbows for Annabel, he had trees that needed to be chopped down.

One day the lumberjack strapped an axe on each of Annabel's hind legs. Then he hoisted a jar of honey on a rope, and the bear climbed right up after it.

When the lumberjack lowered the jar of honey, Annabel climbed back down. As she did, the axes on her legs made short work of the mighty tree trunk and in no time it was ready for the lumberyard. The bear and the lumberjack made a good team, and as her reward Annabel finally ate the honey.

THE JUMPING FROG

THERE ONCE WAS a pet frog who could leap farther than any other frog in the whole state of California.

Before other frogs could even get started, this frog would jump and leap and win every contest. As a result, he had collected many prizes.

One afternoon just before a big jumping contest, confident that he would have no trouble winning, the frog ordered up a heaping pan of southern fried flies.

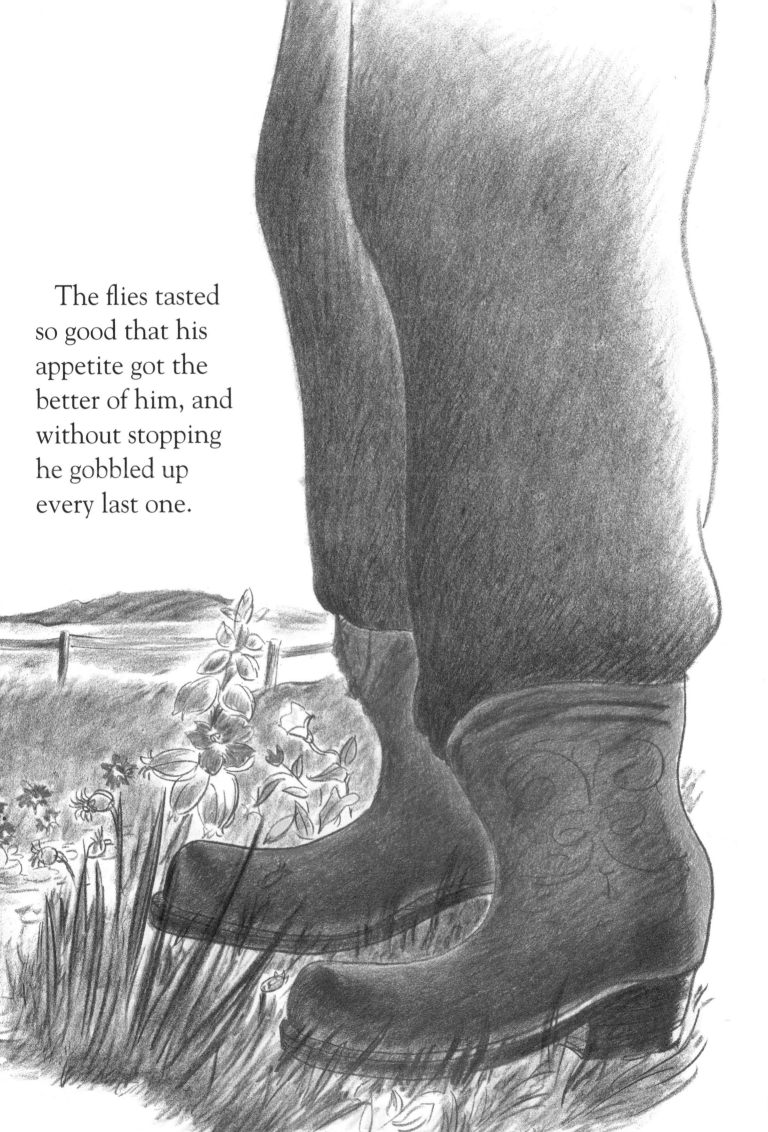

The flies tasted
so good that his
appetite got the
better of him, and
without stopping
he gobbled up
every last one.

Problem was, fried flies are delicious but they are also heavy—and our frog had swallowed too many of them.

When the starting signal came—"one, two, three, JUMP!"—the frog's belly was so full that he could hardly get off the ground.

And now he is no longer champion frog jumper of California.

A TALE
OF
PECOS BILL

PECOS BILL was a cowboy. One day when his horse stumbled and hurt a leg, Bill had to get off and walk for help. He loaded the saddle onto his own back and set out on the long trail to town. On the way, he suddenly saw a ten-foot rattlesnake coiled in his path.

Bill just picked that snake right up. Then he rolled it into a lasso and kept right on walking.

It wasn't long after that, that he met up with a mountain lion. "Well," thought Pecos Bill, "now I can get me a ride to the nearest town." So he put the saddle on the mountain lion and galloped ahead. On the way he spotted a chuck wagon where some cowboys had been rounding up cattle.

Bill was hungry, so he got off the mountain lion and hung the snake around his neck. He ordered a boilerful of hot beans and washed them down with a gallon of boiling coffee. After wiping his chin with a cactus, he asked, "Who's the boss around here?"

A big fellow, at least eight feet tall, had seen Bill ride in with the ten-foot rattler and the wild cat.

He replied,
"Stranger, I was. But
with pals like that, I
reckon you are now."

PAUL BUNYAN
AND
THE LITTLE BLUE OX

EVERYONE knows that Paul Bunyan had a blue ox named Babe. But some folks don't know that Babe had a son called Benny, the little blue ox.

Benny grew very fast. In fact he grew two feet taller every time Paul Bunyan looked at him. He grew so big that one morning he grew right out of his barn!

And Benny was always hungry! One day he
kept bawling and bellowing for pancakes. It took
seventy-eight men just to keep him fed. But even
that was not enough.

Suddenly Benny broke loose and charged into the kitchen. After he ate all the pancakes and all the buckets of batter, he even tried to eat the kitchen stove. But it wasn't until he singed his nose on a hot plate that the hungry little blue ox finally learned his table manners.

PAUL BUNYAN'S NATURAL HISTORY

PAUL BUNYAN had other animals too. Most of these animals are extinct now or maybe only existed in folk tales in the first place. But in the north woods they are still remembered and talked about.

THE RUMPTILFUSEL

This animal looked like a bear but was very thin and could wrap itself around a tree trunk so that it became invisible to hunters.

THE GOOFUS BIRD

This bird didn't care where it was going—it only wanted to know where it had been. It was the opposite of most birds—and always flew backward.

THE PINNACLE GROUSE

These birds had only one wing. In this way they could fly round and round a high hill.

THE HOOP SNAKE

This was a poisonous snake. It would put its tail in its mouth and roll downhill. The only way small animals could escape was to jump through the hoop and keep running.

THE GOOFANG

A very funny fish indeed. It would always swim
backward to keep the water out of its eyes.

THE UPLAND TROUT

A special kind of flying fish that loved nests and did not like water. No fisherman has ever caught one, since fishermen only fish in lakes and streams, and not in the sky!

THE TAR MAN

ONCE THERE WAS a great drought in the forest. The wells went dry and the creeks went dry, and there was no water anywhere.

All the animals in the forest met to see what could be done—the lion and the bear and the wolf and the fox and the giraffe and the monkey and the elephant, and even the rabbit.

Together they decided to dig a well. That is, everybody except the lazy rabbit, who said, "You dig the well, but I'll get a drink from it, all right."

All the animals
worked hard,
except the rabbit,
and soon they
had water to drink. But
the next morning when they
discovered that the rabbit had
been stealing water, the animals
asked the bear to stand watch
during the night.

That night, the bear sat down beside the well.
When the rabbit saw him he began to sing, and
the bear got up and began to dance to the song.
The bear danced so far away from the well that
the rabbit got a drink and scampered away.

The next morning, the animals asked the monkey to stand watch over the well.

When the stars came out that night the rabbit began to sing again, and the monkey danced away from the well. Of course, the rabbit climbed down into the well, got a drink of water, and ran off once more.

Finally, the animals decided to make a tar man to watch the well.

That night, the rabbit crept out of the brambles and sang his song once again. But this time, the tar man didn't move. And the rabbit came closer and closer to have a look. When he touched the tar man he became stuck to him and couldn't escape till the animals found him the next morning.

Pretty soon, the animals began to argue about what to do with the rabbit. "Let's make a new tar man every night," said the lion. "Let's make the rabbit eat pie and cake and sugar till he grows so fat he can't run away," said the bear. After a while they got so busy arguing that they didn't even notice that the rabbit picked himself up and hopped right off into the leaves. But he had learned his lesson and never tried to steal water from the well again.

THE SQUIRREL BOATS

A FARMER had a corn plantation on the banks of the Mississippi River that grew the tallest, biggest corn in all his state. One day he noticed that most of his crop was disappearing. He got up early the next morning to watch the cornfield.

And this is what he saw—

At daybreak, squirrels came from the opposite shore of the river, riding on roof shingles. When they reached the cornfield, each squirrel took an ear of corn and then turned back home.

The squirrels propelled the shingles by swishing their tails in the water—and were soon back across the river with the corn.

The farmer was mighty impressed by the squirrels and figured that if they were clever enough to make boats, they would find a way to get his corn no matter what. The next year, he planted potatoes instead.

THE SINGING GEESE

A FARMER WAS hunting for dinner one day
when he looked up and saw a gaggle of geese.
They were singing, "La-lee-lu, la-lee-lu, come-
quilla, come-quilla, bung-bung-bung."

While he watched the flock, one goose fell out
of the sky. The farmer caught it and brought it
home to cook.

Back home in the kitchen, the farmer put on his chef's hat and sharpened his carving tools. He plucked the feathers from the goose, and as he did, each feather flew out the window.

Suddenly there came a tremendous noise as the whole gaggle of geese flew in through the window. Each one stuck a feather back into the plucked goose. Then they all flew out the window, singing, "La-lee-lu, come-quilla, come-quilla, bung-bung-bung, quilla-hung."

The goose, all her feathers back
in place, lifted herself right off the
platter and flew away with the flock.

SWEET BETSY
FROM PIKE

OH, DON'T you remember
Sweet Betsy from Pike
Who crossed the big mountains
With her brother Mike?

With two yoke of cattle,
A large yellow dog,

A tall Shanghai rooster,
And one spotted hog.

JOHNNY APPLESEED

JOHNNY APPLESEED was a real-life hero who became famous for planting apple trees on farms in the Ohio Valley and other regions of the midwestern United States. Johnny Appleseed spent most of life traveling and he loved the outdoors. Even in the coldest weather, he wore sandals and a homespun coffee sack in which he carried apple seeds.

Johnny Appleseed was kind to all the animals he met in his travels. For instance, if he met a sick old horse, he would care for her until she became healthy again.

Then, when it was time to travel to the next town, he would find the horse a home on a farm where she was sure to have good pasture for her later years.

Once during a cold winter, Johnny Appleseed built a fire beside a hollow log. Then he discovered that the smoke and heat of the fire had disturbed a bear and her cub who were sleeping in the log. Kindhearted Johnny Appleseed put out his fire and slept on the snow outside.

Johnny Appleseed was a real person, not a mythic character. He began planting apple trees in about 1801.

THE KNEE-HIGH MAN

THE KNEE-HIGH MAN lived on a farm and he got his name because that is just about as tall as he had ever grown. One day he said to himself, "I'm going to ask the biggest animal on the farm how I can get bigger too."

So he went to see the horse. "Horse, how can I get big like you?"

"Simple," answered the horse. "You eat a lot of corn and run like me, and soon you'll be big too."

The knee-high man did all the big horse told him—but instead, he got smaller and smaller.

Then he decided to ask the bull. The bull told him to eat grass and bellow and bellow and bellow. The knee-high man did all that the bull told him, but the grass made his belly hurt, and the bellowing made his head hurt, and he still got smaller and smaller.

Finally he decided to see the wise old hoot owl.

"Why do you want to be so big?" asked the hoot owl.

"I want to get big so I can see things far away," answered the knee-high man.

"If you are big enough to climb a tree, then you'll be able to see far away," replied the wise owl. "You see, you don't have to be bigger in size—only bigger in the brain."

THE EAGLES
AND
THE ICICLE

ONCE on a cold winter's morning, a hunter tried to capture a young eaglet high up in a mountain tree. To reach the nest he had to climb a long icicle dangling from it.

Two adult eagles flying nearby—
the mother and father of the eaglets—
saw the hunter climbing up to the
nest.

Of course, the parent eagles rushed back to the nest to protect their young. And our hunter knew he had to escape their angry beaks and claws in a hurry.

So he slid down that slippery icicle so fast that his pants caught on fire! And he never disturbed an eagle's nest again!

DAVY CROCKETT TREES A WOLF

LATE one cold winter night the wind blew so
hard, Davy Crockett took shelter in a hollow tree
trunk to get warm. Soon after, a curious wolf—
the only animal in the forest to be out in such
a cold wind—smelled the scent of a man and
approached the tree.

The wolf circled round and round the tree, sniffing knotholes in order to find out who was inside. But suddenly his long tail became stuck in a knothole. Davy Crockett tried to help the wolf, but it was so cold that, try as he might, the wolf's tail was frozen solid to the tree.

Davy Crockett knew that in a little while the morning sun would melt the ice on the tree and free the wolf. He didn't want a hungry wolf trailing him, so he let the wild creature have the warm tree shelter and he walked off in the snow to find himself another spot.